by Jill Atkins and Andy Elkerton

W

Lucas, Bethany and Noah went camping with Mum and Grandad.

Bethany helped Mum and Grandad put up the tents.
Noah got the tent pegs and
Lucas hammered them into the ground.

Lucas and Bethany helped Grandad
cook dinner on the camping stove.
Noah found an old book beside
Grandad's tent. There was a picture
of a cave on the front cover.
"Look at this," he said.

After dinner, the children sat by the fire.

"Let's read the book that Noah found," said Lucas.

"It's too dark," said Noah.

"I've got a torch in my backpack," called Grandad.

"Thanks, Grandad," said Bethany.
The boys looked on as she shone
the torch on the book.

All at once, red and yellow sparks filled the air.

The light was so bright that the children had to shut their eyes.

After a while, Bethany opened one eye
and looked around.

"Where are we?" she asked.

"It looks like the cave on that book,"
said Lucas. "I wonder if the book
is magic."

"I'm frightened," said Noah.

Bethany gave him a hug.

"It's okay," she said. "I'll look after you."

"Come on," said Lucas. "Let's explore!"

Lucas shone the torch into the darkness.

"Look!" cried Bethany. "I can see some footprints."

"Let's follow them," said Lucas.

The children crept along a narrow tunnel.

Soon they came to a bigger cave.

In the middle of the cave,

there was a chest.

"It's a treasure chest," said Noah.

"Let's see if we can open it,"

said Bethany.

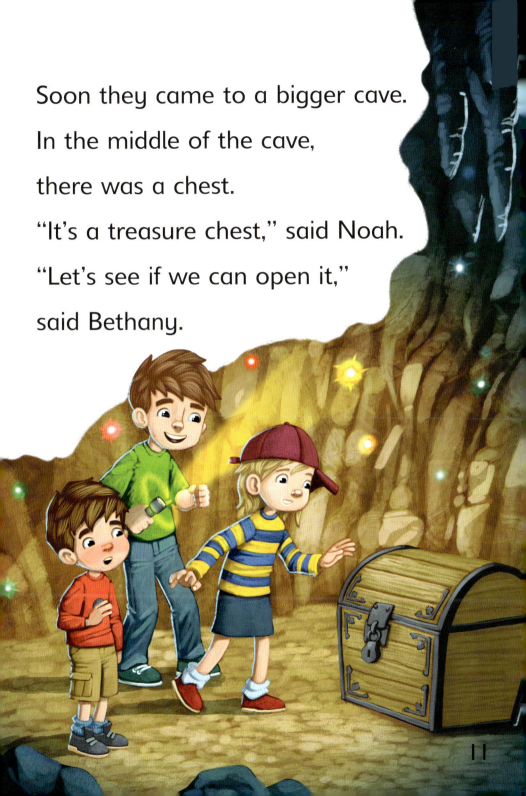

They bent over the chest.

"It's locked," said Bethany,

"and there isn't a key."

Lucas shone the torch on the padlock.

It clicked open and fell off.

"It's Grandpa's *torch* that is magic!"

shouted Noah.

Carefully, Lucas lifted the lid

and the children peeped inside.

There was a message inside the chest.

It said: "Thank you for being so helpful!"

There was also a compass, a map

and a pair of binoculars.

Then Bethany spotted something else
at the bottom of the chest.
"Look!" she said. "It's that book
we were reading."

Lucas shone the magic torch
on the book. All at once, bright red and
yellow sparks filled the cave with light.
The children shut their eyes again ...

... and when they opened them,

they were back by the campfire

with Grandad and Mum.

"We had an adventure," said Lucas.

"We were in a dark cave," said Noah.

"We found a compass and a map

and some binoculars inside a chest,"

said Bethany.

Grandad grinned. "Maybe you can use

them for your next adventure," he said.

Later, before they went to sleep,

they talked about what had happened.

"Do you think Grandad is a wizard?"

asked Noah.

Bethany giggled.

"Maybe he is," she said.

Story order

Look at these 5 pictures and captions.
Put the pictures in the right order
to retell the story.

1

The children found a treasure chest.

2

The children borrowed Grandad's torch.

3

The torch took tham back to camp.

4

The children were in a cave.

5

Red and yellow sparks flew.

Guide for Independent Reading

This series is designed to provide an opportunity for your child to read on their own. These notes are written for you to help your child choose a book and to read it independently.

In school, your child's teacher will often be using reading books which have been banded to support the process of learning to read. Use the book band colour your child is reading in school to help you make a good choice. *Grandad's Magic Torch* is a good choice for children reading at Turquoise Band in their classroom to read independently.

The aim of independent reading is to read this book with ease, so that your child enjoys the story and relates it to their own experiences.

About the book
When the children go camping, they find a book and borrow Grandad's torch to read it. Then they find themselves having an adventure ...

Before reading
Help your child to learn how to make good choices by asking:
"Why did you choose this book? Why do you think you will enjoy it?"
Look at the cover together and ask: "What do you think the story will be about?" Ask your child to think of what they already know about the story context. Then ask your child to read the title aloud.
Ask: "What do you think will happen with the magic torch?"
Remind your child that they can sound out a word in syllable chunks if they get stuck.
Decide together whether your child will read the story independently or read it aloud to you.

During reading

Remind your child of what they know and what they can do independently. If reading aloud, support your child if they hesitate or ask for help by telling the word. If reading to themselves, remind your child that they can come and ask for your help if stuck.

After reading

Support comprehension by asking your child to tell you about the story. Use the story order puzzle to encourage your child to retell the story in the right sequence, in their own words. The correct sequence can be found on the next page.

Help your child think about the messages in the book that go beyond the story and ask: "Who do you think the footprints in the cave belonged to? Do you think Grandad or his torch are magic?"

Give your child a chance to respond to the story: "Did you have a favourite part? Would you like to go on a mysterious adventure?"

Extending learning

Help your child understand the story structure by using the same sentence patterning and adding different elements. "Let's make up a new story about the magic torch. What other places might the torch take the children to?"

In the classroom, your child's teacher may be teaching about recognising punctuation marks. Ask your child to identify some question marks and exclamation marks in the story and then ask them to practise reading the whole sentences with appropriate expression.

Franklin Watts
First published in Great Britain in 2020
by The Watts Publishing Group

Copyright © The Watts Publishing Group 2020
All rights reserved.

Series Editors: Jackie Hamley and Melanie Palmer
Series Advisors: Dr Sue Bodman and Glen Franklin
Series Designers: Peter Scoulding and Cathryn Gilbert

A CIP catalogue record for this book is
available from the British Library.

ISBN 978 1 4451 7149 4 (hbk)
ISBN 978 1 4451 7150 0 (pbk)
ISBN 978 1 4451 7151 7 (library ebook)

Printed in China

Franklin Watts
An imprint of
Hachette Children's Group
Part of The Watts Publishing Group
Carmelite House
50 Victoria Embankment
London EC4Y 0DZ

An Hachette UK Company
www.hachette.co.uk

www.reading-champion.co.uk

Answer to Story order: 2, 5, 4, 1, 3